For my parents, with thanks for a happy childhood —J.O.
For Liberty Bell —C.A.

Originally published in the United States
by Schwartz & Wade Books,
an imprint of Random House Children's Books,
a division of Random House Inc., New York

First published in Great Britain in 2014
by Orion Children's Books
a division of the Orion Publishing Group Ltd
Orion House
5 Upper St Martin's Lane
London WC2H 9EA
An Hachette UK Company

1 3 5 7 9 10 8 6 4 2

The Orion Publishing Group's policy is to use papers that are natural, renewable and recyclable products and made from wood grown in sustainable forests. The logging and manufacturing processes are expected to conform to the environmental regulations of the country of origin.

A catalogue record for this book is available from the British Library.

Hardback ISBN 978 1 4440 1486 0
Paperback ISBN 978 1 4440 1487 7

Printed and bound in China

www.orionbooks.co.uk

Sparky!

written by JENNY OFFILL

illustrated by CHRIS APPELHANS

Orion
Children's Books

I wanted a pet.

A bird or a bunny or a trained seal.

My mother said no to the bird.

No to the bunny.

No, no, no to the trained seal.

I asked her every day for a month, until she finally said,
"You can have any pet you want as long as it doesn't need
to be walked or bathed or fed."

I made her promise.

Then I went to see the school librarian.

Mrs. Kinklebaum (who knows everything in the world)
pointed me to Volume S of the Animal Encyclopedia.

This is what I found:

SLOTH
(sláwth)

Sloths have been known to sleep more than sixteen hours a day. They sometimes hang upside down in trees, barely moving, for long periods of time.

They survive by eating leaves and drinking the dew that collects in them. It is said that sloths are the laziest animals in the world.

SNAKE
(snâyk)

My sloth arrived by Express Mail.

He was about the size of a mediumish dog, with a flat

nose and a monkey face.

My mother wasn't happy, but a promise is a promise, I said.

Sparky, I decided. That will be your name.
I took him outside to his tree.

Sparky went right to sleep.

I made a sign and put it under the tree:

Guard Sloth!
Enter at Your Own Peril!!

It was two days

before I saw him awake.

He didn't know a lot of games, so I taught him some.
We played King of the Castle

and I won.

We played Hide-and-Seek

and I won.

We played Kung Fu Fighter and I won.

We played Statues and Sparky
was very, very good.

That weekend Mary Potts came over to investigate.

Let me show you what Mary Potts is like.

This is a picture of her room:

Before she even took off her coat, Mary said, "Let me see your new pet."

I had some worries, but I took her out to Sparky's tree.

He opened his eyes and looked at us.

Then he closed them again.

I rubbed his tummy, but it was too late.
We stood there for a while, watching him sleep. His fur
ruffled gently in the breeze.

"I feel sorry for you," Mary said. "My cat can dance on her hind legs. And my parrot knows twenty words, including *God* and *ice cream*."

"Sparky knows tricks too," I told her. But she didn't believe me.

The next day, I made a poster and nailed it to the tree outside Mary Potts's house.

All week, we trained in secret. Sometimes Sparky slept through practice and I had to poke him awake.

Sometimes he forgot what he was doing and we had to start again.

Sometimes he took so long to fetch that I went inside
and had tea while I waited.

I was starting to think the poster had been a mistake.

But a promise is a promise.

On the day of the Trained Sloth
Extravaganza, my mother set up chairs.

Three people came to see Sparky perform:
my mother, Mary Potts, and Mrs. Edwin, the
lollipop lady.

(Mrs. Edwin approved of Sparky because he
never ran in the street.)

"Do I look like a ringmaster?" I asked my mother.

"You look very interesting," she told me.

I put a little glitter on Sparky just before the curtain went up.

I kept wishing I had written *Two Tricks* on the poster, instead of *Countless Tricks*.

"Play dead, Sparky!" I said, and he did.

"Roll over," I said, and he didn't.

"Speak!" I commanded.

We all waited.

And waited.

"Speak?" I said.

Sparky looked at me. The only thing you could hear was the wind in the trees.

"He has a very pretty coat, doesn't he?" Mrs. Edwin said finally.

"You can't just invent a brand new pet like that,"
Mary told me. "A pet no one's ever even had!"

My mother came out with lemonade and cookies,
but everyone said they had to be going.

Sparky and I watched them; then my mother
made me put the chairs away.

Afterwards, I gave Sparky a cookie, but he ate
it so slowly that I took it back again.

It was getting dark. I looked at him and he looked at me.

You could hear dogs barking.

I reached over and tagged him on his claw.

"You're it, Sparky," I said.
And for a long, long time he was.